This is Queen Clara. She is a very good queen, and all the people of Story Town love her. The thing about Queen Clara is, she's so very forgetful...

A catalogue record for this book is available from the British Library

Published by Ladybird Books Ltd
80 Strand London WC2R 0RL
A Penguin Company

15 17 19 20 18 16 14
© LADYBIRD BOOKS LTD MMI

LADYBIRD and the device of a Ladybird are trademarks of Ladybird Books Ltd

Printed in Italy

Queen Clara

by Mandy Ross

illustrated by Emma Dodd

One day, Queen Clara was going to open Story Town's new school.

She woke up early and got dressed in her best white vest and her best pink dress.

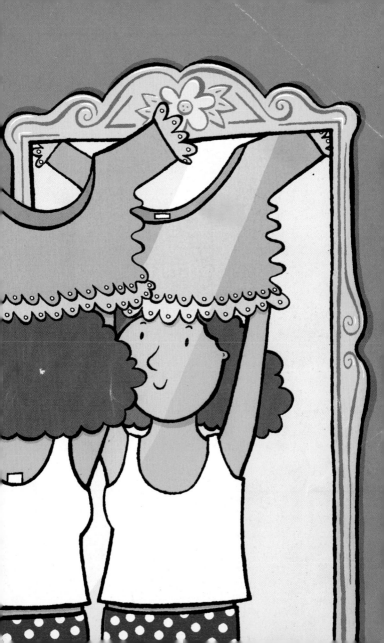

But...

"Oh, crumbs!
Where's my crown?"
said Queen Clara,
and she searched
all over her
royal bedroom.

"Oh, cripes!
Where can it be?"
said Queen Clara,
and she searched
all over her
royal palace.

At breakfast, Queen Clara was very worried.

"Oh, crumbs! Oh, cripes! How can I open the new school without my crown?" she thought.

Just then there was a knock at the door.

"Rat-a-tat-tat!"

"The school is ready, Your Majesty," said Builder Bill.

"But I'm not," said Queen Clara.
"Oh, crumbs! I can't find my crown."

Queen Clara climbed into her royal carriage.

"Is that you, Your Majesty?" asked the coachman. "You look different without your crown."

"Oh, cripes! Perhaps I left it on the train," said Queen Clara...

But the stationmaster hadn't found a crown.

"Oh, cripes! Perhaps I left it at the farm," said Queen Clara...

But Mrs Farmer hadn't found a crown.

"Oh, crumbs! Perhaps someone has taken it to the police station," said Queen Clara...

But no one had handed in a crown to PC Polly.

"Oh, cripes and crumbs! My crown is lost!" sighed Queen Clara, and she started to cry.

But what was that shiny thing under the cushion?

"Crumbs! It's my crown!" said Queen Clara.

"I declare Story Town's new school open!" cried Queen Clara. All the children cheered and shouted.

Builder Bill was very proud.

Queen Clara went home
tired but happy.
"Oh, crumbs!" she said,
"I think I'll sleep with my
crown on tonight, just
to make sure!"

This is Fireman Fergus. He is a brave firefighter and he has a good head for heights. Fireman Fergus has a cat called Tibbles to whom he tells all his Fireman's adventures.

This is Nurse Nancy. She is always neat and tidy and she works very hard looking after the patients at Story Town Hospital.

This is Builder Bill with his yellow hard hat. Builder Bill loves to whistle. He is a very good builder, and his houses never fall down.